CHIMPS DON'T WEAR GLASSES

LAURA NUMEROFF
CHIMPS DON'T WEAR GLASSES

ILLUSTRATED BY JOE MATHIEU

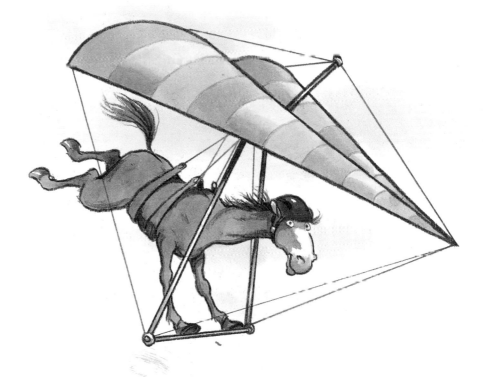

SIMON & SCHUSTER BOOKS FOR YOUNG READERS

Also by Laura Numeroff and Joe Mathieu:
Dogs Don't Wear Sneakers

SIMON & SCHUSTER BOOKS FOR YOUNG READERS
An imprint of Simon & Schuster Children's Publishing Division
1230 Avenue of the Americas
New York, New York 10020
Text copyright © 1995 by Laura Numeroff
Illustrations copyright © 1995 by Joe Mathieu
All rights reserved including the right of reproduction in whole or in part in any form.
SIMON & SCHUSTER BOOKS FOR YOUNG READERS is a trademark of Simon & Schuster.
The text for this book is set in 20-point Esprit Book.
The illustrations were done in pencil, dyes, and acrylics.
Manufactured in the United States of America
10 9 8 7 6 5 4 3

Library of Congress Cataloging-in-Publication Data

Numeroff, Laura Joffe.
Chimps don't wear glasses / by Laura Numeroff ; illustrated by Joe Mathieu.
p. cm.
Sequel to: Dogs don't wear sneakers
Summary: Even though animals don't normally wear glasses, cook, or read, if you use your imagination
you can see them doing these and even more fantastic things.
ISBN 0-689-80150-5
[1. Animals—Fiction. 2. Imagination—Fiction. 3. Stories in rhyme.] I. Mathieu, Joseph, ill. II. Title.
PZ8.3.N92Ch 1995 [E]—dc20 94-20320

Chimps don't wear glasses

And zebras don't cook

And you won't see a kangaroo reading a book.

Horses don't hang glide,

Giraffes don't drive cars
And you won't see a piglet saving pennies in jars.

Mice don't join Boy Scouts

And llamas don't shop

And hamsters don't clean
with a broom or a mop.

Reindeer don't square dance

And seals don't fly kites

And weasels don't travel to see all the sights.

Pandas don't pole vault

And camels don't sing

And you won't find a chipmunk who'll ever be king.

Tigers don't ice-skate
And wolves don't use mugs

And you won't see a puppet show put on by pugs.

Now just close your eyes and draw with your mind.
You might be surprised at what you will find…

Like yaks in tuxedos

And hippos on boats

And otters who ride in parades full of floats.

Or lions who juggle

And squirrels on stilts

And lizards who know how to sew handmade quilts.

Or ferrets who garden

And turtles who dine.

But tell me what you see. It's your dream—not mine!